Bonnie Ramona of Oz

For

Florence and Buzz
with my best wishes
Charles Wells
and love from
Ann Stewart

BONNIE RAMONA

by Charles Wells

with drawings by Ann Street

BACKBONE PRESS

Nashville

OF OZ

Published by
Backbone Press
Box 58153
Nashville, TN 37205-8153
email:backbone@backbonepress.com
http://www.backbonepress.com

ISBN 0-9646112-1-X
Library of Congress Catalog Card Number: 97-94130

Printed in the United States of America

CONTENTS

For my first friend
Clyde DeLoach Ryals

ACKNOWLEDGMENTS

I wish to especially thank three persons:

Gary Gore—master of graphic design, who deserves all
our praise for the beauty of the book itself.
Ann Street—distinguished portrait artist, whose drawings
so enliven the text.
Ann Wells—my critic, my editor, my publisher, and to my
great good fortune, my wife.

Charles Wells

PREFACE

In the two years since *Dear Old Man*, my first nonmedical book, was published, friends and acquaintances have often asked if I am at work on another book. When I proudly tell them that I am writing a book about my dog, Ramona, responses have been varied, unpredictable, and at times even humorous.

True dog lovers, a clear minority among my acquaintances, respond quickly and without hesitation: "Wonderful, I want a copy," or "I can't wait to read it." Pleasure, satisfaction, and complete understanding shine through.

Those whose affection for dogs is less complete react in a more measured fashion verbally, though their uplifted eyebrows and widened eyes often betray their true thoughts. After a pause, "About your dog, you say? Tell me about it."

Ignoring their look of incredulity and attending to the show of interest expressed in their words, I try to explain. "It's a group of essays about Ramona and me, about our life together. In some ways it may be more about me than about Ramona. It deals really with the nature of our relationship." Usually by the time I get to the part about the nature of the relationship, my listener has either become glassy eyed or has begun not so furtively to look around for a means of escape.

Finally, there is that group, fortunately not large, that actively dislikes dogs, though its members are hesitant to admit this publicly. It's like fessing up to a dislike for motherhood and apple pie and baseball. I've heard the most varied responses from this group, but I think it's epitomized by the individual who abruptly and rather challengingly asked, "What's the plot?"

In our family, we have a tradition that always brings smiles to our faces. Whenever any one of us announces a plan to do something that the others of us consider totally outlandish, whenever we're at a total loss to make any sincere or considerate or affirmative response, we reply, alone or in unison, "How nice!"

It's a response I suspect many of my questioners would have made, had they been aware of our family tradition, when I told them I was writing a book about my dog. I hope, however, if they overcome their doubts and actually read through the book, that they do not mutter to themselves in our peculiar fashion as they finish the last page, "How nice!"

I hope that members of all three groups will come to read this collection of essays, and I hope that each reader finds them touching and meaningful and genuine. And finally I hope that when the last page is turned, each reader will think, "How nice," or even "How very nice," using those simple words in their true and heartfelt meaning.

CW

Bonnie Ramona of Oz

The name on her birth certificate (kindly supplied by the American Kennel Society for a fee of seven dollars) is Bonnie Ramona of Oz. It specifies further that she is a West Highland white terrier, that she was born on April 14, 1993, and that she is the offspring of Kay's Bonnie and of Storyland Wizard of Oz. Her name is apt, because she is both beauteous and fair, yet her playful nature would make her much at home on that yellow-brick road cavorting with Dorothy and Toto.

She would be much at home on that yellow-brick road.

I still don't understand the longing for a dog that arose in me so strongly a few years ago. Certainly it was a longing neither I nor those who know me would have predicted. Most likely it was the remnant of some childhood dream, forgotten but never completely erased. As a boy I'd asked for a dog, perhaps because I thought it was expected of me, and once my father even brought home for me a bright, frisky little puppy. He was soon gone, however, before I even had time to name him, after he threw up all over the back seat of my father's new automobile during our first Sunday afternoon drive. I don't recall feeling bereft or even deprived. Almost certainly I didn't press for another, for my indulgent parents would probably have supplied it.

Clearly though, some spark of desire smoldered on, because shortly after Ann and I were married I bought her a dachshund pup, which we named Bonnie to rhyme with the name of her parents' dog, Honey. Then followed Roly Poly, another dachshund, and Frisky, a black Labrador retriever, which stayed at the side of our sons and daughter until they were away in college. These dogs owed their allegiance, though, to Ann and the children, and not to me. When Frisky died at the age of twelve, Ann and I agreed that life without a dog isn't necessarily bad, especially as one grows older.

Even so, some gnawing yen must have lingered, because, several years ago, with no apparent cause, I began to talk to Ann about my getting a dog—someday. Some months later, I bought a large, illustrated book that de-

As a boy I had asked for a dog, perhaps because I thought it was expected of me.

scribed the different breeds of dogs, and, after much delib-
eration, announced that I had settled on a West Highland
white terrier. Still, many months passed before I actually set
out to buy a puppy.

I considered only the two females from her litter. Both
were funny looking, straggly-haired little creatures, bearing
few hints of the beauty that was to come. But when I knelt
down to greet them properly and called for Ramona, for I
had already decided on her name, one waddled over and
began licking and nibbling at my fingers. I knew then that
she was Ramona and that she had chosen me.

I was sixty-four years old and had never before had a
dog of my very own. Was I too old to adjust to having a new
member of the family? Was I energetic enough to be able to
care for her properly? Was I perhaps temperamentally un-
suited for this new role as master to a young puppy?

The answer to all three questions must have been "no,"
for she and I have accommodated nicely to life together.
She has brought me delight such as I had thought I would

not find again in this life. She has made me feel like a boy again. Each morning when she awakens, she regards me with a trust so certain it is almost palpable. Each time I return home, I hear her little squeals of delight before I can even open the garage door, and she greets me with a boundless joy that humans can almost never show. And in the evening too she brings me peace as she lies sleeping in my lap while I read.

Ramona isn't perfect, of course, either in her behavior or in her conformation. She's spoiled beyond measure, for she wants constant attention and can be annoyingly persistent about getting it. She has a brown spot on her tail, and her ears don't stand up as perkily as should those of a champion of her breed. On the other hand, she's endlessly playful, full of good humor, and she makes us laugh. Is it any wonder I find her perfect?

She's spoiled beyond measure.

She has brought me joy in abundance, but she has also been my teacher, as I have been hers. She has taught me lessons that I already knew but had never learned. Chiefly, she makes me aware each day how truly important are the joys we often regard as insignificant. She has taught me about deeper things too, such as love. I never dreamed it would be possible at my age to find room in my life for a new love, and especially a love as intense as is mine for this furry little creature. I've come to realize that the heart has no limits in its capacity for love. I even suspect that the unfolding of a new love leads to growth of the old ones as well, the new invigorating the old.

In my more uninhibited flights of fancy, I sense Ramona may be a messenger sent from heaven to help me learn about important things such as love and joyousness and devotion and adoration. Sometimes I even imagine she's an angel in disguise sent to walk beside me as I try to find my way through these years. When I think on it, such fancies are too wild for me to take seriously, yet I know I do.

I don't believe there is anything amiss, however, when I envision a magnificent "Adoration of the Shepherds" which I might commission some contemporary artist to paint for

I never dreamed it would be possible at my age to find room in my life for a new love, and especially a love as intense as is mine for this furry little creature.

the side aisle of our church. In the picture I see myself painted, as were patrons of old, kneeling among the shepherds with Ramona at my side before Mary and the Christ Child in the manger at Bethlehem. Our figures are fixed there forever in awe and adoration as we join with the angels and the shepherds in singing "Glory to God in the highest, and on earth peace, good will among men."

Ramona Goes to College

Ramona came to us in the early summer several years ago, when she was only two months old. At such a tender age, she obviously had not developed even the most rudimentary habits essential to civilized living. Accordingly we began at once to tutor her in certain necessary and expected behaviors. Although at first she appeared uninterested, she gradually began to show evidence of a keenness for learning that excited Ann and me as new parents. We both realized, however, that we lacked the basic qualifications needed to assist her in achieving her full potential, and we began to think of her broader educational needs.

Each of us inquired of our friends and of Ramona's professional caregivers as to which school might be appropriate for her. After several independently recommended the Superior Dog College, Ann telephoned to arrange admission, and although it was summer vacation time for students and teachers, she finally reached the registrar. This kind lady relieved our apprehensions by assuring us that the College would unquestionably accept Ramona, and that indeed Ramona was the first to enroll in the beginners' class for the following January (attainment of the age of six months being one of the requirements for matriculation).

We were delighted that Ramona had been accepted by such a well recommended institution but were distressed that she must wait until January before her formal education could begin. Ramona was, to us, so obviously precocious that the age requirements should have been waived for her. What if she found the subject matter too juvenile and

We were delighted that Ramona had been accepted by such a well recommended institution.

thereby lost her excitement for learning because of the need to conform to the learning curve of less intellectually adept canines? Our entreaties fell on deaf ears, however, and the registrar refused to waive the age requirement and approve her for early admission. Although we were disappointed by the decision, we continued to talk enthusiastically about the school whenever we were in Ramona's presence, hoping thereby to keep her excitement alive.

The waiting months seemed endless but, still, Ramona, on her own, made quick strides toward maturity. She found the Christmas season particularly exciting as she was the only one of our family to be visited by Santa Claus, our children having become adults long before. Santa, and our family, surprised her with a variety of squeaky and gnawy-chewy toys, all of which she chewed and gnawed and threw about, producing a cacophony of sound. Although the Beasleys had kindly included Ramona in their invitation for Christmas Day brunch, we had declined for her, fearing that the combination of Ramona and the Beasleys' several dogs might dampen the holiday spirits of the other guests. We need not have been concerned lest Ramona miss us when we left for the Beasleys. She was too engrossed in her cornucopia of Christmas toys even to notice our departure or return.

Late in December, a large packet of instructional materials arrived from the College, detailing preparations to be made for the initial class. We were to measure Ramona for the uniform collar and leash that all pupils were required to wear in class. Further, we were to bring quantities of paper towels and plastic bags in anticipation of accidents, and per-

haps even small rugs for the pupils in case the floors proved too chilly. Finally, we were to present ourselves promptly at seven o'clock on the first Monday evening in January at a large Metro school building for the first of ten evenings of instruction.

Arriving early for the first class, we were surprised to find the parking lot already crowded with cars. A mass of people and dogs, mercifully attached to each other, milled about nearby. It seemed that many different classes for all levels of instruction had been scheduled that evening, some of the pupils being enrolled in advanced postgraduate courses. From the moment we drove into the parking lot, Ramona had been a small white furry bundle of enthusiasm, straining on her leash in every direction at once, eager to make new friends. My words and sharp pulls on the leash made no impression on her, and I realized that school had been delayed almost too long. As I looked about us, however, I saw that virtually every other dog was behaving in exactly the same fashion. Unfortunately, I could not distin-

Some of the pupils were enrolled in advanced postgraduate courses.

guish between those dogs already in advanced courses, and those just beginning their studies.

Ramona found herself in a class of small dogs, approximately twelve in number. I was pleased to note that all appeared to be of good breeding and to have come from good homes. In addition to Ramona, there were two other Westies, three shelties, a bulldog, a Shih Tzu, a Maltese, two Scotties, and a schnauzer. The last, aptly named Blockbuster, struck the only discordant note in the group, as he was disagreeable and loud, and never followed one of his mistress' commands throughout the course. His embarrassed owner spent her time apologizing for Blockbuster's behavior and reiterating to anyone who would listen that she worked out of town and left him with sitters several days a week.

I must admit that Ramona herself was inadequately socialized with her own kind. Ann, our children, and I were her only companions during her formative months. Even when we had guests, they were more likely to be people than dogs. Thus, Ramona was accustomed to people, but not to animals. In this new and exciting academic environment, her only desire was to play with her classmates. In moments, her interest in learning had evaporated.

Her teacher, Miss Able, was not about to let Ramona get away with such as that. Hearty and forthright, Miss Able, a woman of uncertain age, was clearly accustomed to being in charge. Her perfect sheepdog, Bo, always stood beside her, waiting to follow her next command. Sometimes I considered Bo's presence an affront to us all, though I never discussed my feelings with other parents. It was Miss Able's opinion that dogs, like horses and men, must be broken to their masters' wills. She clearly was not destined to be a shepherd gently leading her flock, nor would she ever be the sort of person who considered her dog a near human companion to whom she would confide her most tender thoughts. I was not so much resistant to this approach as I was uncertain that Ramona could be broken to any person's will, even that of Miss Able.

Instructions were that pupils were to learn one new response to command every week. While this response would be demonstrated and practiced at each class, mastery would require much homework. Miss Able insisted that owners should practice with their pupils at least fifteen to thirty minutes every day. Those unable to commit that much time should not expect success. Each of the first nine class sessions would teach new responses, while the tenth and last session would be a rigorous examination testing each pupil for each of the assigned lessons. No pupil would receive a diploma without attending and participating in the final examination. Clearly the curriculum was demanding, and expectations high. Ramona and I had come to the right college.

Clearly the curriculum was demanding.

The first evening, pupils were to learn "to sit" on command. Miss Able taught parents exactly how to lift their dog's forequarters and to push down on the hindquarters while saying in a firm, but not harsh, voice, "Sit!" Ramona evinced little interest in what I was doing, hardly acknowledging my command and posturing maneuvers, as she quickly resumed whatever posture she chose as soon as I removed my guiding hands. She ignored me as she turned her entire attention to the other dogs. I spent most of the evening tugging on her leash to pull her away from the other students, as our teacher had instructed us, in order that she not interrupt their learning experience. The class seemed interminable. I could scarcely believe it was only eight o'clock when Miss Able announced that instruction had concluded for the evening. We left with her parting admonition to practice *every day* ringing in our ears.

During the next week, Ramona and I were compulsively faithful in our practice. We worked almost every day on her studies. Despite our diligence, however, Ramona didn't follow my commands any more consistently on the following Sunday than she had on the preceding Monday evening when we had been given our instructions. I was discouraged.

Nor had my efforts been limited to simple practice maneuvers. Our *hundmeister* had instructed us that our charges would learn more quickly if we immediately rewarded their proper response to commands with a tasty morsel. As she had suggested grilled frankfurter slices as a favorite reward, I had visited Hill's Food Store to select the proper ones for Ramona. Since we'd not had a frankfurter in the house for years, I was amazed at the variety offered, and barely able to choose the most tasty from the selection laid out before me.

Having returned home with the proper frankfurters, I began what was to be the weekly ritual for the College term—cutting the frankfurters into slices three-eighths of an inch thick, cooking them in the microwave exactly one minute, and then freezing them so that I might quickly retrieve and thaw them for each practice session. Our instructor had informed us that there was a skill in presenting the reward at just the right moment after the correct performance. This was a skill I never acquired, for I could not see that Ramona followed my directions any more consistently when I provided rewards than when I did not. When I reflect, the only predictable consequence of the reward effort was that my pockets became extremely greasy and our cleaning bill increased.

Despite the disappointments of our practice sessions, Ramona and I faithfully returned for our second class and our second maneuver, which was to "stay" on command. It was, understandably, a difficult task to teach Ramona to "stay" when she had not yet mastered the command to "sit," but we persevered. Our pattern of weekly tutelage had become well established. In class, we performed a near charade of the week's new task, while out of class we returned to the most basic commands. As the weeks went on, new tasks seemed to tumble out on top of each other—staying while the master walked away, down to the prone position, staying in the standing position when approached by another, walking to heel, walking in a figure eight.

During our sessions at home, we spent a lot of time on "sit," with Ramona's girth increasing, the result of the tender bits of frankfurter I was so furiously feeding her. Occasionally she would sit and look up at me with a most fetching smile on her face, but seldom when I had commanded her to do so. She seemed particularly unimpressed by walking to heel, believing no doubt that it was not only her right, but indeed her duty to lead. All my commands of "Don't pull, Ramona," accompanied by fierce backward jerks of her leash, fell on deaf ears and a supple neck.

As the weeks passed, the classes became more melancholy. There were dropouts—one of the Westies, a fine looking English bulldog, the Shih Tzu. Their absence went unexplained. Were they experiencing the same problems as Ramona, and had their masters simply given up? Or was the class too elementary, so that the dogs had no need for classes to learn such basics? Certainly the three shelties in the group seemed to need nothing more than a single demonstration to master a skill. Only Blockbuster and Ramona appeared to remain oblivious to all instruction, to have learned nothing.

Was the class too elementary, so that the dogs had no need to learn such basics?

As time for the examination neared, tension among masters and pupils palpably increased. Several masters began taking up classtime to inquire exactly what would be required for graduation. With each repetition of the requirements, I was flooded with more and more anticipatory anxiety. I realized too that I must be unconsciously transmitting my anxiety to Ramona herself, as her brow grew furrowed with concern.

As time for the examination neared, tension increased.

Most of the week before the examination I spent in perplexity. Our practice sessions were continuing even more rigorously than before, but were producing no evidence that Ramona's learning curve was turning upward. What should I do? Should I subject Ramona to the embarrassment of a failed examination? On the other hand, might she not feel worse if I withheld from her even the opportunity to compete? Finally my compulsiveness won out. We had signed Ramona up for ten sessions; we would attend ten sessions.

I was clearly not feeling my best when examination

night came around. My heart was racing, and a decided queasiness had settled in my epigastrium. The examination was to be so public—there would be none of the privacy of examination papers returned with the grade concealed inside. Indeed, a number of teaching assistants had been brought in especially to grade our performances.

As preparations for the examination began, instructors gave each team of dog and owner a number to be prominently displayed, and deployed us at intervals around the walls of the gymnasium. We performed the stationary commands in unison, but had to carry out the maneuvers in motion one by one, walking down the middle of the room, with all eyes looking carefully for any misstep. I felt like the Miss America contestants must feel when they parade down the boardwalk at Atlantic City.

About halfway through the examination, I sensed that Ramona was performing rather better than usual. Even so, it seemed to me that the other dogs were much quicker to obey than was she.

Finally we arrived at what I knew to be the evening's final hurdle—the three minute "stay" in the down position. So far as I could recall, Ramona, unless asleep, had never remained still for three minutes in any position in her entire life, certainly not in her practice sessions with me. As the maneuver began, three minutes seemed an eternity. Blockbuster, as expected, was the first to break "stay," after only about fifteen seconds, and most of the others faltered at some point during the exercise. To my surprise, Ramona stayed until released, along with the three always perfect shelties. At last it was over. We had all survived the examination.

The judges retired in great solemnity, leaving us parents a bit giddy and euphoric. Without our instructor to restrain us, we allowed the dogs to mingle and socialize, and even they seemed to realize that something momentous was over and done.

At last it was over. We had survived the examination.

Finally the judges returned, and our instructor, Miss Able, took the floor to announce the results. She first awarded several dogs yellow ribbons, no particular sign of distinction, for they were presented to each dog who merely participated in the examination. She next announced the recipients of gold and red ribbons, to signify graduation with some honor. Since there had yet been no mention of Ramona, I feared she had somehow been forgotten in the tabulations. As I was raising my hand to inquire, I heard Miss Able say, "And the blue ribbon goes to Ramona, the only pupil in this class to make a perfect score."

Ramona appeared not at all astounded.

Ramona beamed. I beamed. The class was astounded. I was astounded. Ramona appeared not at all astounded.

Moving outside into the cold night air, I was expressing to Ramona my pride in her performance, but she began to pull and tug ahead as usual, heedless of my compliments and unresponsive as usual to my commands of "Don't pull" and "Heel." Why, I wondered, when she is so obviously capable of following commands, should she continue to be disobedient? Search as I would, I could reach only one conclusion.

Ramona is willing on occasion to permit me to appear her master in the eyes of others. On the other hand, she wants to make it quite clear to me that I am her master only when and if it pleases her. Our life together is smoother when I keep this in mind.

3
Ramona's First Friend

Ramon came to us long before we adopted Ramona. While working in my flower garden one afternoon, I looked up to find him standing atop the six foot brick wall that surrounds the garden, surveying all that lay below in a measured way, as though it were his kingdom.

Ramon was a medium sized cat, of a rich golden color, sleek of coat, and beautiful in posture and conformation. He sat calm and serene, the clone of some ancient Egyptian god, miraculously reincarnated in Nashville, Tennessee, in the late twentieth century. I neglected my duties for several minutes, on my knees in admiration.

Unattended cats are not unusual in our neighborhood, their owners treating our leash law for cats with the contempt it deserves, so I gave him little thought, except to notice his beauty. Returning to my duties, I was surprised a few minutes later to find him on the ground, walking carefully through the vinca towards me. He showed none of the hesitancy, even skittishness, that cats usually display when and if they deign to approach a stranger. His step was slow, certain, measured, as though he had no question as to how I would respond, as though he knew already that I would be his faithful subject. As he approached, I could hear him purring softly. Reaching my side, he bowed his head, and I reached out instinctively to stroke the back of his head and neck, this clearly having been his objective. Coming closer, he circled my ankle and leg, embracing them in the arc of his back. After this brief expression of affection, he settled

Unattended cats are not unusual in our neighborhood.

down to observe my labors. When I looked up again, he was gone.

Afterwards, when I walked or drove about the neighborhood, I saw him occasionally, as he rested under a bush or walked alone, always with an appearance of purpose. If I were taking a walk, he would come when I called, though he would stay with me only briefly. I noted that he wore no collar or identification tag, and that he never appeared in any predictable place, and it dawned on me that this beautiful, friendly animal might be homeless, that he had no human family taking responsibility for his well-being. That burden fell on him alone.

It dawned on me that this beautiful, friendly animal might be homeless.

With time he visited me in my garden more often, where I would find him sunning himself on the wall or on the steps. He was always friendly, affectionate, even loving in his behavior. I even grew to hope that he might adopt me as his responsible adult, as another cat had done years earlier. To promote this feeling of belonging, I named him

"Ramon," a rather special favor from me, as I had chosen the name "Ramona" for a dog I hoped to find and adopt one day. Until the dog Ramona appeared, it seemed appropriate to address her potential surrogate, a male cat, as Ramon.

On some visits, Ramon would greet me with a series of "meows" instead of purrs, and when he did this, I would bring him milk, and later, tins of cat food which I had begun to buy specially for him. Unhappily, my efforts to ingratiate myself with him further came to naught. While he would sometimes take a sip of milk or a morsel of food, he never accepted my gifts with enthusiasm. Though he still called on me from time to time, he came infrequently and stayed for only a few moments. Never able to find a key to unlock the store of loyalty that surely lay hidden inside him, I tried to accept failure gracefully, to realize that he might allow no mere mortal to change his cadence. He chose to grant me only occasional closeness, for which I became thankful.

When we adopted Ramona a few months later, I began

to take her on a leash for walks through the neighborhood. We often encountered Ramon, usually taking his ease on the mulch under a convenient shrub. From the beginning, Ramona was attracted to Ramon. I didn't know whether she perceived him as playmate, father, or god, but every time she spied him, she strained at her leash to reach him. Ramon was, simply put, her first friend.

Ramona's feet whirled about as she strained against her leash.

Every time she glimpsed him, Ramona's feet whirled about as she strained against her leash, eager to play with this entrancing creature, to sniff and nudge him at will. He permitted this only briefly, soon arising carefully and walking away with a stately stride, as I continued my efforts to restrain Ramona's boundless enthusiasm.

As Ramona grew—to say she matured would be an exercise in wishful thinking—she began to temper her approach to Ramon. As she did so, Ramon tolerated her for longer periods. Occasionally, he rubbed his neck and back against her as he did with his human friends, often startling her so much that she would jump away. He would follow us for a while, but always at a rather formal distance, so that his interest in her would not appear obvious.

For a while, Ramon sported a bright green collar.

Over the following months, I walked less often in the neighborhood, so had fewer encounters with Ramon. Still, he always greeted me cordially, and on a few occasions he walked along beside me for a short distance. For a while, he sported a bright green collar that looked especially vivid

against his golden fur, but soon that was gone, the only tangible evidence that others might have been concerned about him. He continued to be a solitary, regal creature, independent and self-reliant, beholden to none, apparently having no need for steady companionship, whether feline, canine, or human. I fancy this didn't reflect any basic distrust of others, but rather revealed enormous self-sufficiency.

Recently, when he appeared after a long absence, Ramon give me cause to hope he might be changing. As Ramona and I were coming home after a morning walk, we met him as we neared our house. The two creatures—sleek, self-sufficient cat, and furry, enthusiastic dog—proceeded to execute the ritualized choreography that characterized their meetings, then parted when each had reached its limits of tolerance for the other. Ramona and I continued on our path to the house, up the steps to the front door. Ramon followed only a pace behind, meowing all the way, even as Ramona and I went into the house, even as the door closed

Ramona and Ramon parted when each had reached its limits of tolerance for the other.

behind us. A moment later, I looked outside to see him sitting beside the front door. Minutes later, he was still sitting there, his measured meows parting the morning stillness. I wondered if he might be hungry, though his body appeared robust, his fur sleek. Had his wandering perhaps led him to hard times?

Concerned for Ramon, I hastened into the kitchen to pour a bowl of milk, and then moved out onto the front porch to set it before him. When he showed some slight interest, I returned inside, so as not to intrude. Soon curiosity won out over discretion, and I returned to peer out a side window to observe. The bowl of milk sat in its place, apparently untouched, and once again Ramon had disappeared from sight.

Ramona and Me

I have never been a man absorbed in the mysterious workings of my own mind. Although in my psychiatric training I had a brief experience in self-examination under a noted psychotherapist, I never had any yen to submit myself to the long, arduous, perhaps unending process of psychoanalysis. Thus I never expected to find the continuing puzzlement that I have experienced in the relationship that has come to exist between me and Ramona, between Ramona and me. It has caught me unawares, and I find myself

She, like Will Rogers,
has never met a man
she didn't like.

trying to understand it. I list again and again all the factors that draw me to Ramona, and I search for those that might attract her to me. Then I tot up the scores, hoping each time for some kind of balance.

"How do I love thee? Let me count the ways." In Ramona's case, I grow weary of counting.

She is endlessly affectionate. No doubt she would be content to spend each day's twenty-four hours either asleep or being cuddled, by me or another family member, or by anyone who would gently rub or scratch her chest. In truth, aside from food and water, she asks for little more. Although she may have her preferences, she, like Will Rogers, has never met a man she didn't like. On first meeting Ramona, each of our friends feels singled out for her special attention. Only by observing her response to others does one come to realize that her affection is cast extravagantly about her, on the just and perhaps on the unjust alike.

She is not totally unselfish in the broadcast of her regard, for she clearly expects a loving response in return, and

Faced with a rebuff,
she redoubles her
efforts.

appears puzzled when it is not forthcoming. Faced with a rebuff, she often redoubles her efforts, to the obvious discomfort of the one who has spurned her overtures. Sometimes it's difficult to dissuade her from persisting in her efforts to amuse. At other times she redirects her overtures to acknowledged friends whose response will be predictable. When I have petted her for a period of time I deem sufficient and then announce, *"Enough,"* she is likely to turn her back and move a step or two more distant, only to renew her efforts after a pause that she considers appropriate.

There is somewhere within her an apparently inexhaustible reservoir of good will, at least for human beings. I have never seen her snap or bare her teeth or bark at any person in her presence, not even when she is seriously provoked, as when a toddler pulls her ears or when I inadvertently step on her paw. She can be ferocious toward other dogs, big or little, but clearly for her, humans exist to be loved.

She is also extraordinarily playful and at times downright funny. She can make a game of almost any small object she finds on the floor—one of her toys, a sock, a tennis ball. First she brings the object to me, and it is then my job to wrest it from her mouth and throw it away, so that she can fetch it and bring it back to me, whereupon we repeat the process. Sometimes it seems there will be no end to these repetitions. At others, after only three or four times, she ignores me when I throw the object, moving on to something else without even a farewell.

Occasionally, when we are outside, she will begin what we have come to call her "romps," whereupon suddenly, without warning, she commences running in wide circles around me at a furious pace. Abruptly she changes course, heading straight for me, only veering off course at the last possible moment to avoid collision. When she tires of running, and of my laughter and cries of encouragement, she falls at my feet or else runs up our steps to sit before the front door, panting and with a big smile on her face. Either action signals the end of the performance.

She is also endlessly forgiving. When I speak to her perhaps too harshly about some bit of outrageous behavior,
when I fail to take her with me for a drive and she badly
wants to go, when I withhold additional popcorn because I
think she's had enough, or even when I leave her in a kennel for a week or two while we travel—no matter what, it
seems she always forgives, coming back to me with undi-
minished signs of love and affection, licking my hand as her
token.

*I often feel inadequate
beside her.*

Lastly, she trusts me unreservedly. When she sleeps beside me in my chair in the evening, no one could doubt that
she is in Beulah land. If I held her in my arms, I believe that
I could take her into a burning building with no sign of
protest. Such trust is disquieting, but it is also gratifying,
giving purpose to our days together.

With all these gifts, it's no surprise that I love her. Indeed, I often feel inadequate beside her, and I wonder if she
may not have been sent to teach me many of the things
about which I have so long remained in ignorance. Open af-

fection, playfulness, forgiveness, trust—have not all these been difficult for me to own? To think that the guide who would lead me is not even a little child but a little dog!

In this relationship, the giving cannot be all one-sided, else it would not be worth recording. Although she gives to me liberally, she must perceive me to be giving as well. What is it that I give to her?

First, I too give affection in many ways. While my displays may not be as ebullient and inexhaustible as hers, she recognizes the pleasure with which I greet her, the certainty of the pats and rubs that I administer just when she wants them, the lap and chair that I offer her to lie beside me in the evening, the way I delight in her very presence. All of these can be wordless, of course, but I talk to her as well, usually trying to modulate my voice so that it touches her as softly as do my hands.

She knows too that not only do I care for her, but that I also take care of her. I walk outside with her each morning and night, serve her food with its special treat of cottage

The giving cannot be all one sided, else it would not be worth recording.

cheese each morning, and put medicine in her eyes each morning and night. I take her for walks, and for drives in my car, both of which she enjoys enormously.

Beyond all that, if I cannot offer her true security, I offer at least the illusion of security, which, if we are fortunate, may be just as valuable as the real thing. When I am about, she need no more be on the alert, on the lookout for possible danger. She can give over these responsibilities to me, and rest without caution.

Ramona and I give and are given in return. We have learned to live together in harmony without one being in control of the other. We realize that we cannot please each other all of the time, and relish the time that we do. We respect each other. We love each other. The balance between us in secure.

Ramona Abed

Even before I fetched her from the kennel, I bought Ramona a "pet carrier," one of those perforated plastic carrying cases with a handle that one sees so often in airports as travelers transport their pets to or from planes. At two months of age, Ramona was a very small puppy, so I had bought the smallest size available, hoping that she would feel snug and secure inside it. My mentor at the kennel had assured me that all dogs love to sleep in such relatively Spartan quarters when they have been brought up to do so,

and insisted that I should begin acclimating my puppy to her carrier that very evening. In fact, I began even earlier, placing her there for the journey home. She whimpered most of the way, but I attributed this more to the pain of separation from her sister than to any dislike for her carrying case.

As we discussed Ramona's bed that evening, Ann and I agreed that the empty case was too spare for our new little puppy, so we put a soft, downy towel inside for her to sleep on. Amazingly enough, the kennel owner's advice then proved to be true. Ramona seemed to recognize the carrier as a place to sleep, and she curled up and placidly dozed off almost directly after being put inside. The pattern continued. Frequently I found her still sleeping when I went to fetch her in the morning. With time and a little maturation, she began even to walk into the carrier on her own when I would open its wire-mesh door, a habit I sought to reinforce nightly by putting munchy treats inside with her.

She began even to walk into the carrier on her own.

The carrier served other purposes as well—for trips to

the veterinarian, for weekend visits to our mountain cottage two hours distant, even for a few longer journeys of several hundred miles by car. In all these situations she appeared comfortable and happy in her portable little home. She grew, of course, so that after some months I had to buy a larger carrier for her, but she seemed equally secure in her new model.

All went splendidly for about eighteen months, but then I began to notice subtle changes in Ramona's behavior. When I would open the little door for her to enter in the evening, she would hesitate ever so slightly before moving inside. Though I sought to remedy this by augmenting her treats, she continued to hesitate, to dawdle along the way. Finally I was forced to conclude that Ramona no longer found it safe or comfortable to be closed up for the night, especially in a room so far removed from our bedroom. Indeed she became positively resentful as we went through our nightly ritual.

What to do? Ann and I discussed this at great length,

All went splendidly for about eighteen months.

then finally arrived at a complex but sure solution, one certain not to increase our pup's insecurity, but instead to pro-
vide comfort by our presence. The plan: we would buy a
large, comfortable dog bed for our Ramona, aiming for it
eventually to rest in our bedroom so that we could supervise
her more closely. But to lessen the shock she would doubtless feel at any sudden change, we would begin the process
by placing the new bed close beside her carrier in the garden room, where she had always slept. If all went well, if she
kept to her new bed for the entire night, then we would
gradually begin to increase its distance from the pet carrier,
moving it away ever so slightly each night until finally it
should reach its appointed spot in our bedroom. With such
attention to detail, how could anything go wrong?

To implement our plan, we spent some time selecting
the appropriate bed. We found one of medium size, with a
soft, nearly plush cushion for its mattress. Next we searched
for the proper moment to introduce our special little dog to
her future bedstead. Feeling that an evening not long after

we had purchased the bed was auspicious, I initiated the plan. Beginning in the accustomed place of the garden room, I placed the new bed beside the pet carrier, set Ramona's treats atop the new cushion, and gently lifted her in my arms. Settling her lightly on the cushion, next to the treats, I then sat and rubbed her chest carefully to relax her for sleep. After determining I'd left on a light so she wouldn't be frightened, I returned to our bedroom and lay down to read.

I'd not even had time to find my place in the book when I heard the sound of a little bell drawing close, and there was Ramona, the bell on her collar jingling as she stood beside our bed, peering up at me with what was surely an inquisitive look. Though she appeared not at all perturbed, I was concerned that she might be fearful, so I picked her up, walked into the garden room, and once again placed her on her little bed. After I had repeated this process several more times, and still Ramona appeared at my bedside, I gave up. While I had been growing ever more frustrated, Ramona had appeared to be enjoying herself immensely. Finally the only solution struck me. I picked up the new bed and brought it into our bedroom, whereupon Ramona jumped into it, and immediately fell asleep.

Her aim is to sleep not just in the room with Ann and me, but to put herself right between us in our bed.

Thus began the struggle that still continues between us and Ramona. Clearly her aim is to sleep not just in the room with Ann and me, but to put herself right between us in our bed. So far Ramona is still battling forward in her contest. Soon after she and her dog bed moved into our room, we realized, as did she, that she could jump onto our bed alone and unassisted. Before long, as soon as the alarm rang in the morning, she leaped onto our bed, insinuating herself between Ann and me, then quickly going back to sleep. Even in retrospect, I think it's understandable that we were usually too sleepy at that early hour to insist on her leaving, particularly since I usually get up earlier than Ann does, and I reasoned that if I thoroughly awakened Ramona, she might then wake Ann.

Ann and I usually like to read in bed for a while each

night before turning out the light. Cleverly, Ramona quickly learned to jump onto the bed while we were reading, and again placed herself between us. Quietly attentive to us though she was, she didn't seem upset that she didn't have a book of her own. When I concluded my own reading, I was becoming tired of getting up to put Ramona back on her own bed, so that with not much effort, I taught her to jump up whenever I said, "Ramona, time to go to bed." At first eager to obey my command, she soon assumed a reluctant posture, rising up slowly, walking more and more hesitantly to the side of the bed, jumping down only when I insisted, "*Ramona*—Bedtime!"

By now she has learned to pace ever more slowly from her warm spot in the middle of our bed to its edge, from whence she fixes me quizzically with her gaze, as if to say, "How could you do this to me? Don't you know I'll be all by myself over there? Don't you love me anymore? I'm too small to jump off this high bed." All this I hear in her gentle gaze, but if I then say simply, "Come on, Ramona, you can make it," she will jump down and make her way reluctantly to her little bed, eyes downcast in resentful submission.

I'm well aware, though, that the night will probably come when I'm simply too sleepy to say, "Come on, Ramona, you can make it," and Ramona will settle down to spend the night contentedly between us, and then of course to spend every night thereafter between us as well, immensely proud of the contest she's finally won. I try to stay on guard to defend us, but I know that, inevitably, no defense can stand permanently against Ramona's resolute doggedness.

No defense can stand permanently against Ramona's doggedness.

6. Ramona at Beersheba

In my prayers, which I try but don't always succeed in offering daily, I say my thanks for "our wonderful house in Beersheba." In truth, it's only a simple cottage sitting on the rim of the plateau, off to itself in a spot where peace and quiet surround it. I go on to pray that we may keep it a place of "rest, respite, and repose, a refuge and a retreat from the world, a place where we may go when we are weary, there to regain our faith and vitality." Feeling as I do about the place, it's small wonder that I go there as often as opportunity arises, even if it be for but a single day. Some friends find this hard to understand, failing to grasp how the few hours in Beersheba could possibly justify a drive of almost a hundred miles each way. To me, though, the time is always well spent, and I never regret the effort.

Indeed, the time in transit can be just as satisfying as is the time there. Ann often goes with me, even on brief day excursions, and we find the journey gives us a space of time such as can almost never be found at home or anyplace else, time when we can talk without interruption. As we drive, we can discuss our views, talk out problems, or make plans with a thoroughness and lack of haste that we can seldom arrange otherwise. When I make the trip by myself, the opportunity to think without interruption for an hour and forty minutes, each way, is a luxury that I rarely allow myself in other circumstances. I accomplish much of my planning and even writing, in my mind, during these trips.

Actually, nowadays I hardly ever go alone, because Ramona usually comes along. She dearly loves an automobile ride, so for her, riding for an extended period is an unparalleled treat. She usually senses that a journey is in the offing long before it's time to leave. Since trips back and forth to Beersheba almost always involve taking things to our house or bringing them back home, it's virtually impossible to prepare for the journey without catching the eye of such an observant dog.

Whenever she senses that a departure is imminent, Ramona stations herself in expectation close by the door to the garage, so that every time we crack the door open even a little, she nudges her nose through so as to get a look at the car. When I see her there, peering expectantly, I command her to "stay," and she does so, for a moment. But too many "stays" quickly exhaust her patience, and then we notice that she has left the house, and has bounded close to the car, where she stands, not at all patiently, beside the rear door, waiting for me to open it for her. When I have done this, she springs into the car, and assumes *her* place—hind legs planted firmly on the back seat, forelegs on the divider in front, head and ears erect in anticipation. Once she is thus stationed, her patience apparently knows no bounds, for she will stand in place, almost motionless, for as long as

Whenever she senses that a departure is imminent, Ramona stations herself close by the door.

is needed for the loading, seemingly as happy to be there as were the car in motion.

While *en route*, she usually maintains her stance, at least while we are still in town. The sight of another dog along the way will, however, elicit from her squeals of delight that reveal all her longing for canine companionship, squeals that inevitably end in quiet whimpers as she realizes once again that her wish to play with the dog thus glimpsed is not to be gratified. When she sees a dog, she usually leaps toward the window, pawing it and pressing her nose against the glass in bitter frustration. Sometimes a car will attract her attention, especially, of course, should the car carry another dog as passenger.

She is not much attracted to bucolic scenery, and once we reach the open road, she quickly loses interest. She then turns her attention to our car's interior, which she explores on every trip as though she'd never ridden there before. Every corner and crevice must be explored, her nose twitching constantly, her eyes fixed on sights our human senses cannot perceive. Ventilation ducts catch her fancy, and she

will stand nearly motionless, her nose almost touching the
vent while her fur is blown backward in the breeze. At var-
ious times, she is sure to assume her place once again as she
paws my right arm gently with her right forepaw, a well recognized signal that she wishes me to scratch or pat her
chest. If I do not comply, and sometimes to do so in traffic
is improvident, her signals become more insistent. She will
desist only if I say "Enough!" with a sure ring of authority.
After a while, even such pleasures as these lose their savor,
and she curls up and goes to sleep.

I doubt that she has ever been awake to see the truly
beautiful scenery that surrounds us as the road lifts upward
to the top of the plateau. But the moment the car turns onto
the short graveled street leading to our house, she is fully
alert and standing at the window, uttering little squeals of
excitement that continue to crescendo until the car stops at
our house.

I can never open the car door fast enough for her, for
she leaps over me and claws at the door before I can turn off
the motor. Once outside she quickly settles into the ritual of

Every corner and crevice must be explored.

I spy her digging a hole, eager for an animal morsel that could delight only a terrier.

not so systematic exploration with which she occupies herself on each visit. While in the city we have no sizable yard that she can explore safely free of her leash, in Beersheba there is ample space, much of it left to grow wild, and she can explore to her heart's content. I fancy that Beersheba is her Garden of Eden, filled with every possible beauty and delight. She spends most of her time sniffing, nose to the ground, busily intent upon a world known only to her. Occasionally I spy her digging a hole, seemingly eager for an animal morsel that could delight only a terrier. Because we are still unsure about her homing instincts, when she is too long out of my sight, I will call her. As she scurries into view without much delay, I tell her, "That's okay." Then she knows she is free to resume her quest. The only apple in her Garden of Eden is the bluff where the land drops off precipitously to the valley that lies beyond our house. There she seems to have no fears, but I hope that the repetition of my barked "no's" may eventually limit her explorations of this forbidden area.

While she rambles, I am, as a rule, just as intently occupied with some garden project. If she feels that I have neglected her too long, she might pay me a visit, standing silently scrutinizing my work until I pause and turn my attention back to her. Not infrequently she finds a comfortable spot in the sun where she takes a nap. She sleeps far less in the daytime in Beersheba than she does at home, as though unwilling to squander a single moment in such an endlessly absorbing setting. From time to time she has adventures about which we can only speculate, as when she returned to the house last weekend, covered in mud from nose to tail, smiling and apparently much pleased with herself.

Rarely, but so pleasantly, opportunities may arise in Beersheba for her to play with her friends. As I have hinted, Ramona is an uncommonly gregarious creature, though she has few occasions for peer play in the city. In Beersheba, on the other hand, our next door neighbor has a little Maltese dog, and Ran, who often stays in our guest house, may come

Ramona is an uncommonly gregarious creature.

with his two dogs, of uncertain breeding but wonderful temperament. Down Backbone Road, her friend Erich spends weekends with his parents, Ann and Bob, and she and Erich often sup together. When any or all of these dogs are visiting, Ramona pays attention to little else and spends long periods playing with them. Since she is undoubtedly the most energetic and enthusiastic of the group, I am always grateful for their tolerance of our Ramona, who believes in unending play.

More often, though, Ramona and I spend the day alone together, caught up in our separate worlds but each comforted by the presence of the other. When I have completed my day's chores and begin preparations for the return, she is again alert and at my side, seemingly as stimulated by the prospect of the drive home as she was by our coming in the morning. She jumps back into the car as soon as the door opens, and she takes her place in the center, all patience once more while I arrange around her the objects that we are taking home.

Whether I've been in Beersheba for a day or for several days, I never leave without regret, without wishing I might stay just a little longer. Ramona appears untroubled by such sentimentalities, and she is again aquiver in anticipation of our departure. However, her eagerness fades quickly into exhaustion after her active day, and she usually falls asleep quickly and remains so for the entire trip. I cannot sleep, of course, but I am aware of a pervasive sense of ease and of a mellowness that were missing on our drive up to Beersheba earlier in the day. These are the gifts that our day in Beersheba together has brought us, peace for me and for Ramona.

Ramona and Mabel and
Buttercup and Lucy

As I should have anticipated, Ramona's arrival was not greeted with unalloyed joy in our household. Although I claimed her as my very own puppy and planned to take general responsibility for her upbringing, I was still working long hours in my medical practice, and had only a short time at home each morning and evening. It was therefore clear that Ann must bear the daily burden of Ramona's upbringing. Inasmuch as Ramona gave no hint of even being aware of the civilized disciplines expected of dogs in our society, the task was no small one.

Although Ramona appeared to be an intelligent little puppy, she evinced no interest in learning to control her bodily functions. She came to us in June, and throughout the summer months her learning curve remained horizontal, while Ann's frustration curve rose ever nearer vertical. We almost dreaded the approach of September and its long planned vacation trip, as we knew that we could not take Ramona with us, and that our only recourse was the kennel. Shortly before our departure, I took her there with great reluctance, almost certain that, without our constant loving attention, she would be miserable, and even worse, without our prompting, she would forget her modest learning accomplishments.

Upon our return, I immediately rushed to retrieve her from the kennel where I found her as happy and enthusiastic as she had been two and a half weeks earlier. In other ways, however, she returned to us a changed puppy. Almost at once she was housebroken, and both of us began to regard her with a new delight.

Several months later, much to my amazement, Ann suggested, almost as an afterthought, that she might like to have a dog of her own. With time she expanded on this idea. First, she said, Ramona could benefit from having a companion. "She's so extraordinarily gregarious," Ann mused, "yet she is seldom in a situation where she can play with other dogs." Another Westie might be the best choice, as Ramona would doubtless be most comfortable with another of her breed. And further, might it not be great fun to have two dogs around, just as the McLeods have always had two Skye terriers? "We'll call her Mabel," Ann announced with finality.

Ramona would benefit from having a companion.

Her choice of names surprised me. Somehow Mabel did not, on first consideration, seem a felicitous choice. It is not mellifluous as are "Ramona" or "Sarah," which the Nischans named their dog, or "Augustus," as Marnie Wright named hers. Nor does it carry with it any sense of great affection, as would "Precious" or "Honey." In fact, it is rather sharp, even harsh. Might this choice reflect some still unresolved resentment toward Ramona? After all, Ann had never openly acknowledged any great affection for her. Well, it was not my business. Clearly Ann has a right to name her dog whatever she pleases.

In time, Mabel became for us Ramona's imaginary play-mate. Ann and I began to talk of the things Mabel and Ramona would be doing together much as though she were al-ready with us. As Ramona's first birthday approached, we had serious discussions about whether this might be the proper age at which to introduce a companion into her life. Reluctantly we agreed that it was probably a little early, that we should wait until she was a little older, a trifle more ma-ture.

Talk of Mabel dwindled over the next few months, and then, rather to my surprise, Ann began to talk of a puppy named Buttercup. When I asked what had become of Mabel, she said that Mabel no longer seemed an appropri-

ate name for her puppy, and so she'd decided to call her Buttercup instead. Buttercup indeed sounded right. I could easily picture Ann with her dog Buttercup, whereas I'd had
trouble doing so with Mabel.

Even in absentia, Buttercup became a member of our household.

As had been the case with Mabel, Buttercup, even in absentia, became a member of our household. Although there
was no certainty about when she might attain a physical
presence among us, there was no uncertainty about her
coming. Ann intended to have her Buttercup. But still, Ramona's second birthday came and went without Buttercup.
As we considered the upcoming summer, the only time to
adopt a puppy, we knew that it was already too crowded
with other commitments for us to take on another new
obligation.

We missed Buttercup, nevertheless. She'd been with us
in our imaginations so long that it sometimes seemed as
though she'd been taken from us. We thought ahead. Might
not the spring of Ramona's third birthday be the perfect
time for Buttercup to arrive? By this time, Ann had become

very open in acknowledging her love for Ramona. She'd even covered a low bench in her home office upstairs with a soft quilt, so that Ramona would have her own special place beside her as she worked. Now she could look forward to having both dogs with her there.

Just at this time, our son Harwell and his wife, Jenny, began to speak of getting a dog, as they had perceived a void in their life which only a dog could fill. Jenny had always adored Ramona, who regarded her with equal adulation, so a dog seemed natural for her. Rational arguments concerning possible impediments of their work schedules and finances fell on deaf ears, and soon both Harwell and Jenny were immersed in canine reference books, searching for the breed that would most perfectly answer their needs. We were especially pleased when they announced that their choice was a West Highland white terrier.

Having assumed that they did not plan to acquire their dog until sometime in the future, we were caught off guard when they telephoned only a week or so later to announce

Rational arguments fell on deaf ears.

that they had purchased a two month old Westie they had named "Lucy." Not just any Westie, she had been sired by Ramona's littermate, and thus was her niece. Their satisfaction was obvious, as was ours. Yes, they had Lucy at home with them already; but no, we should not come over just now to see her. She needed time alone with them to grow accustomed to her new situation before being introduced to other family members.

But it wasn't long before they invited us to meet Lucy. Ann and I arrived at the scheduled hour, without Ramona, who, we all agreed, might overwhelm the young puppy. And when we first glimpsed Lucy, there she was, a tiny clone of Ramona except that her ears stood up straight whereas Ramona's had always flopped. We could hardly recall that Ramona had ever been so small. It was easy to recall, though, that she had been just that lively, as we observed Lucy running around the house almost without ceasing, pausing for an instant now and then to greet an adult, or trying again and again to jump up on a chair, apparently not discouraged by her repeated failures. We could occasionally entice her to let us hold her for brief moments, during which her tongue sought ceaselessly to lick our hands or face. She was lovable and laughable at the same time. We would easily come to love Lucy too.

A week later, Harwell suggested he and Jenny bring Lucy over to introduce her to Ramona. The three of them arrived at the appointed time, along with Lucy's carrying case, to be held in reserve lest she need a respite from Ramona. At once Lucy and Ramona fell all over one another. The floor was a blur of white furry bodies, racing and tumbling, mouths agape in mock anger, producing growls which only their owners could recognize as affectionate rather than hostile. From room to room they raced, only to collapse in exhaustion, and to rest for a moment before returning to their games. Although Lucy was no more than a fourth of Ramona's size, she held her own in vigor and feistiness. At the end of a half hour, Lucy's parents concluded she'd

The floor was a blur of white furry bodies.

had enough excitement for the evening, and took her home.

Since then, Lucy has paid us regular visits, and no one is sure whether she or Ramona is the happier for them. Sometimes Harwell and Jenny drop her off for an hour or two while they run errands that might bore Lucy. Other times, she comes to spend the day. On these occasions, after the two dogs have played incessantly, Ann has been known to sit on the sofa, holding a dog on each side and calling "Time Out," so as to keep them apart until their panting breaths and racing hearts subside. Else, she fears, they would play until one or both reached absolute exhaustion. Even so, when Lucy leaves, Ramona heads straight to her bed for a long nap.

Lucy has clearly filled a void in Ramona's life. No longer need she long for a companion of her own kind, for not only does she have another Westie to play with, but also she has a kinswoman for companion. With this happy turn of events, talk of Mabel or Buttercup has ceased temporarily.

Speaking realistically, Ann recognized that it might be a trifle late to begin training a new puppy of our own this year. Still, she noted that next year we could find Buttercup in the spring, and have her housebroken in the fall. "After all," she acknowledged, "Lucy will probably take to a puppy a little better when she's older."

To lessen any lingering disappointment for Ann, Jenny and Harwell brought us a white furry stuffed dog, almost exactly Ramona's size, and closely resembling her, even down to her smooth nose and bright eyes. We call her Buttercup. We are occasionally startled and amused when we walk into the living room, where she currently has her place on the loveseat, and think, just for a moment, that she is real.

But still Ann dreams on. Recently she told me of a perfect, tiny puppy she'd seen while shopping, a puppy so small that its owner held it in her arms. When she approached and inquired, the pup's owner pronounced it to be a "Teacup Poodle." It had seemed happy and contented, agreeably allowing Ann to pet and hold it.

"I think I'd like a dog that I could carry around with me everywhere, a dog which would always be beside me," Ann announced. And then, after a long pause, she added, "I believe that when we get a puppy next year, she's going to be a Teacup Poodle."

Ramona and Her Health Care Providers

I have always held that good health is next to godliness, so it was appropriate that one of the first things I did after Ramona came to us was to take her to see our veterinarian for a physical examination. Dr. Campbell of the Hillsboro Animal Hospital had cared for our Labrador, Frisky, through her degenerative arthritis, and I was glad that he was willing to accept Ramona as his patient.

Dr. Campbell is a smiling, friendly man who exudes an air of competence. It comes as no surprise that he gets along as well with people as he does with dogs. Ramona clearly recognized that he was fully in charge in his examination room, and she submitted to his probing and poking with just enough resistance to let him know that she was an independent spirit. To my delight, he pronounced her quite fit, and we went on our way rejoicing.

Thereafter we saw little of Dr. Campbell for a long time. Ramona had regular checkups and inoculations, of course, but she was a healthy puppy and had no need of further medical attention. Even so, it was a comfort just to know that Dr. Campbell was there.

Then, sometime in Ramona's third year, Ann asked if I had noticed that she appeared to be squinting, specifically out of her left eye. Now I have always believed that most malfunctions of the human body will go away if one just leaves them alone and gives them time, and I could see no reason why the same should not be true for a dog. Accordingly, I chose not to look at her left eye for several days in hopes that whatever was wrong would go away. Ann kept

Ramona appeared to be squinting.

after me, though, and when I finally did scrutinize Ramona's left eye, I had to acknowledge that indeed it appeared to be reddened, and that Ramona was squinting.

At. Dr. Campbell's the next morning, he quickly recognized that she had conjunctivitis. Then he instilled fluorescein into her eyes, and when, in the darkness, he shone light on the left eye, even at a distance I could see that she had a scar on her cornea—a corneal abrasion. Had she injured it in some way? Not that I knew. Has she been seen scratching the eye? Not by me. Armed with an antibiotic and a soothing ointment to be instilled into the eye twice daily, I went home to administer her nursing care. I was instructed to bring her for reevaluation in ten days.

I had feared that Ramona might resent or resist frequent treatments, but she appeared to relish them, initially at any rate. They must be relieving her discomfort, thought I. In fact, she did seem to be squinting less, and I was optimistic when we returned ten days later. Yes, Dr. Campbell allowed, she was better, but not completely healed, and if this persisted for long, her cornea might be scarred permanently. She must see an ophthalmologist without further delay.

Within a day or two, Ramona and I were on our way to keep an appointment with Dr. Laratta, veterinary ophthalmologist, in Nolensville, a small, truly country town several miles south of Nashville. How such a prominent veterinary ophthalmologist came to locate in Nolensville remains a mystery. Somehow, whenever I'm in Dr. Laratta's presence, such a question seems trivial, too insignificant to be asked. Thus I remain in ignorance.

Within a day or two, Ramona and I were on our way to keep an appointment with Dr. Laratta, veterinary ophthalmologist.

Of Dr. Laratta's prominence, however, there could be no doubt. The waiting room was packed with visually impaired pets and their worried owners. Only the fact that Ramona appeared so much healthier and livelier than any of the other dogs kept my optimism from turning to despair. Our turn soon came, and we found ourselves once again in a darkened examining room. Yes, there was indeed a corneal abrasion, but it appeared to be healing, and permanent scarring was unlikely—certainly a welcome message.

Dr. Laratta moved swiftly to solve the problem. In the light now, he inserted short strips of litmus-like paper under each lower eye lid and timed to the very second the period they were to remain there. Voila! Here was the answer. On the right, the paper had turned blue for several millimeters, on the left probably not even one millimeter. Ramona's left eye was producing almost no tears, and even on the right, tear production was faulty. Ramona had "dry eyes"—*kerato-conjunctivitis sicca*. She would need medicines instilled into her eyes twice daily to stimulate tear production and prevent further scarring—and would probably need this for the rest of her life.

Thus began a daily morning and bedtime ritual of eye treatments which punctuate our lives together. Initially Ramona seemed eager for her treatments and would quickly jump up beside me on the chair or sofa where I was sitting to perform her treatment. With time, however, the allure of treatment has clearly faded, and sometimes I must coax her with all my persuasive powers just to get her to jump up—

and if I am sitting on the sofa, she may scurry down to the opposite end from whence I may even have to retrieve her.

Our visits to Dr. Laratta have dwindled to twice yearly. Each time he measures her production of tears, thus providing me visible evidence of her improvement. Nonetheless he, Ramona, and I are well aware that the continuation of her improvement depends on her treatments being kept up regularly and permanently.

Otherwise Ramona has been an exceptionally healthy dog. Recently, though, our daughter, Ann, while petting her one evening, found a small nodule on her back. I examined it, and because it appeared painless and was freely movable, concluded it was most likely a lipoma, or a small fatty tumor, and of no danger. Nothing need be done, I decreed. The two Anns, mother and daughter, perhaps recollecting my failure to diagnose Ramona's dry eyes, insisted that she must go to her physician.

(My firm conviction that most ills will go away if they are neglected long enough led me, some years ago, to ignore my appendicitis until it had ruptured. It is possibly well for mankind that I chose psychiatry as my specialty rather than the more traditional medical specialties.)

Dr. Campbell quickly diagnosed Ramona's nodule as an infected cyst, and advised that surgery be performed that same afternoon. Ramona came home soon after the surgery, looking more than a little groggy, but otherwise no worse for the experience. By the next day she was her usual energetic self, and by evening she was able to greet our dinner guests with her expected verve. Dr. Campbell called a few days later to report that the pathologist had discovered the cyst to be benign, as he had predicted.

Ramona came home a little groggy.

Once again, Ramona is in good health, truly next to godliness, and with the assistance of Dr. Campbell and Dr. Laratta, we hope to keep her so.

Ramona Abed: Part II

And it all came to pass as I had foretold. It transpired, however, much more rapidly than I had anticipated.

While Ann and I were away for two weeks in August on a driving trip through the Northeast, Ramona remained at home with our daughter, Ann. We had thought this to be a perfect solution, as Ann and Ramona are very fond of one another, and there would be no need for Ramona to be placed in the kennel. It so happened, however, that, while

we were away, our son Harwell was also out of town, and
Ann invited his wife, Jenny, to stay with her in our house for
a few days, bringing with her, of course, their dog, Lucy.

Lucy has slept on Harwell and Jenny's bed almost since
infancy, so of course she continued to sleep with Jenny during their stay at our house. Understandably, Ann was distressed even to consider Ramona's sleeping alone when, just
across the hall, her niece Lucy was enjoying the warmth of
Jenny's bed. Ramona pleaded her case silently, but with such
persuasiveness and pathos that Ann finally acceded. Thereafter, Ramona slept each night on Ann's bed.

Surprisingly, after our return, Ramona adjusted well to
the changes, and we encountered no problem in persuading
her to resume her previous habit of sleeping in our room in
her own bed. All went well until the fateful time, a month
later, when I had to leave town on business. I'm sure this
provided the exact moment for which Ramona had been
waiting. Silently but again convincingly she pleaded her

case, this time with Ann, Sr., and again she was successful. Even so, upon my return, she compliantly resumed sleeping in her own bed.

Then, only a few nights later, without much thought and with no identified proximate cause, instead of telling Ramona to go to her own bed as usual, I told her nothing at all. She stayed on our bed and slept there, as she has done each night since. I should like to believe that she pleaded more eloquently that night than before, causing me to lose all resolve, or that Ann had insisted on it, but neither is the case. I should also like to believe that I relented entirely to give Ramona pleasure and comfort. That too is not true.

I've come to realize that I like having Ramona close beside us each night. When she snuggles close to one or both of us as is her habit, her presence is satisfying to me. When I wake in the night, I find it comforting to reach out and touch her gently, as I do Ann, so as not to waken her, finding myself reassured merely by her sleeping presence. I've

I find myself reassured merely by her sleeping presence.

been surprised to recognize that what I had perceived as a gratuitous gift to Ramona was actually determined by my own wants rather than by hers. Fortunately, our wants happened to be identical. It has been a welcome gift for both of us.

Ramona Speaks

Anthropomorphism: an interpretation of what is
not human in terms of human characteristics

The longer my life is blessed with Ramona's presence, the more I find myself succumbing to the allure of anthropomorphism. While anthropomorphism is not a sin in itself, it is almost certainly an egregious error in thinking, one which perhaps I should admit only with contrition. I must confess however that it has become one of my most comforting habits, never failing to bring me enjoyment, and I have no intention of trying to break it.

"Why are you
scolding me this
way? You know I'm
just a little puppy
and can't help it."

As with so many habits, its origin was so trivial that I can't even recall it. Most likely it began when Ramona was a small puppy. When I scolded her for some minor infraction, she would look up at me with solemn face and sad eyes, as if to say, "Why are you scolding me this way? You know I'm just a little puppy and can't help it." Thus I interpreted her demeanor, sharply rapping myself over the knuckles for my harshness. From such commonplace incidents strong habits are born.

When she rushes to my side each morning at the first sound of the alarm, when during the day she wanders away and at my call comes racing back into my arms, when she dances and spins about me upon my return home each evening, surely Ramona is telling me that I am the most wonderful person in her world. When she looks stolidly at me while I eat munchies without sharing them with her, when she stands, feet planted, staring at Ann and me as we leave for an evening's outing, when she appears nonplussed each night as I tell her that it's time to jump off our bed and into her own, doubtless she is thinking, "How could they treat their best friend this way?" Although this is certainly fanciful thinking on my part, surely such thought patterns are common among those closely bonded to their pets.

Were I though to describe only such commonplace examples, I would merely be skimming the surface. For at times when she sits, calm and serene, head erect, nose slightly elevated, eyes fixed on some object none of us can see, surely she is sensing herself a queen, ruler of all she surveys, awaiting only the opportunity to grant a favor, to show her graciousness, her condescension. Sometimes she stays by me while I work in the garden, her intent look conveying an intense and hitherto unrevealed interest in matters horticultural, the tilt of her head questioning my placement of a particular plant or the severity of my pruning. Then she is my mute but willing Egeria, advising by her every gesture. And in the evenings when, having tired of

She sits, nose elevated, eyes fixed on some object none of us can see.

her continued demands for attention, I finally proclaim, "Enough!" and she turns her back to me in a plenitude of self-sufficiency, surely she is telling me, "I can get along without you very well."

From this point, I need only a leap of faith to translate her inchoate vocalizations into intelligible dogspeech. If she wakes and, after stretching, makes a sound closely resembling "ahwee," she is indicating that she is still sleepy and wants to be left alone. When the sound of gravel under our tires signals that we are approaching our mountain home, her high-pitched squeals doubtless tell us, "I can hardly wait to reach this place where you let me run free." When she looks out the window of our house and spies a rabbit calmly sitting in the square beyond, her unbridled yelps demand that we let her out to chase that rabbit as she was bred to do. Or, long before we can hear the approaching footsteps, she runs to the front door, barking ferociously, saying, "I warn you of danger, complacent humans!

I need only a leap of faith to translate her vocalizations into intelligible dogspeech.

Be prepared to defend yourselves!" All this ceases, fortunately, the moment the door opens as she rushes to greet all callers with love and affection, whether they be friends or strangers.

This communication is far from one-sided. I often find myself talking to Ramona, both aloud and sotto voce, and, by some mental legerdemain, I usually maintain the illusion that she is responding to me in a meaningful way. Sometimes I talk to her as I would to a child. For example, when we are working in the garden together, I may tell her the names of the flowers I am planting, what the blossoms will look like, and why I am placing them just so.

Other times though, I talk to her as though she were a sage. When we are alone together in the car for a trip of an hour or two, I find myself advising her of some conundrum I am dealing with, of some choice that must be made. She appears to listen intently, and I am free to carefully consider the problem from every angle, to wrestle with every possibility. It is as though I am talking with an oracle of old, knowing that whatever the response, it will come to me as a riddle that I must interpret, but which will lead, nevertheless, toward some resolution.

It is when engaged in such flights of fancy that I sometimes begin to wonder if I have not taken anthropomorphism too far, if indeed I have not allowed it to exceed the limits of reasonable thinking. Usually I can put such questions aside, figuring that the satisfactions of my thinking seem to exceed its liabilities most of the time. A recent incident has, however, forced me to confront this question anew.

It happened when Ann and I were sitting on the porch of our mountain cabin having breakfast, enjoying the cool air and the sight of the valley beneath us. The only sounds came from the songs of birds hidden in the trees and the whir of hummingbirds hovering near the three feeders we have for them there. Suddenly we observed a single, unusu-

Suddenly we observed a hummingbird approaching.

ally small hummingbird approaching, the hum of its tiny fluttering wings barely audible, while, even louder, we heard it make a distinct clicking noise. Ann, looking down at Ramona sleeping at our feet, smiled as she said, "If Ramona were a hummingbird, that's the kind of noise she would make."

It took me a few moments to catch on. Ann too was falling into anthropomorphism. If Ramona were a hummingbird!

A Day at Miss Kitty's

Not long after Ramona came to us, we began to hear tales of an establishment called "Animal Attractions." It was always described in glowing terms—a wonderful boutique of the latest canine fashions, a gourmet shop filled with treats sure to please the palate of even the most discriminating doggie, a styling salon that excited raves even from the most fastidious of owners. To tell the truth, despite the uniform praises, Ann and I were not at all sure Animal Attractions was the right place for Ramona. We have always perceived her as basically a plain and simple girl, elegant in her simplicity perhaps, but one not likely to be at ease in a high fashion ambiance such as that portrayed at Animal Attractions.

Accordingly, many months passed without our taking Ramona there. Then Ann found that she must be away for a few days, leaving Ramona and me alone. I could not conveniently go from my work back home several times each day to carry Ramona outside for her responsibilities. Yet I was reluctant to put her in a kennel for the several days, not the least because I should be so lonesome at home in the evening with both Ann and Ramona away.

What about the possibility of day care for Ramona? One of us recalled hearing that Animal Attractions offered day care, and "yes," they would be glad to accept her for the few days needed.

I took her early one morning with some trepidation. Ramona was uneasy as well.

I took her early one morning with some trepidation. Ramona was uneasy as well, clearly reluctant to follow me into the small undistinguished dwelling that then housed the establishment. When I fetched her that afternoon, somewhat to my surprise, she appeared exceedingly happy. The staff assured me that she'd had a wonderful day and that they had greatly enjoyed having her. I thought that either they were telling me the truth or else, that they had been very well trained. Whatever the case might be, it was a good sign. The following morning, she showed no hesitancy whatsoever, happily jumping out of the car and scampering quickly up to the front door.

Not long thereafter we received a notice that Animal Attractions, rechristened "Miss Kitty's Bed and Bath," was moving to a new location, to bigger quarters on a large fenced lot providing space for the animals to play outside. From then on, and without our planning it, Ramona has become a habitué of Miss Kitty's. She's there regularly for her bath, irregularly for grooming, occasionally for day care, and from time to time for boarding when we are out of town. In fact, if Ramona were human, Miss Kitty's would be her club—a place for meeting her peers, rehashing the problems of the day, playing a few hands of gin, perhaps partaking of a gin or two.

As the morning journey to Miss Kitty's has been repeated, Ramona has become quicker and quicker to recognize her destination. Time was when she would not be aware that she was going to Miss Kitty's until she saw the bright red door. Now she begins to squeal with delight shortly after we turn off the interstate, a full half mile from Miss Kitty's, squeals that accelerate in volume until we stop in front of the red door.

By then, she's pawing the door of the car to get out. There is no restraining her. Once out of the car, she races to the door to get inside, and once in, she rushes about and begins clawing the next door that leads to her heaven, the grooming room where all the dogs congregate. I must hurry to open all doors for her. The staff has learned that I must satisfy her insistence even before she is checked in.

What goes on behind those closed doors, I can only imagine.

What goes on behind those closed doors, I can only

imagine. Clearly for Ramona, it is a very special place, probably her favorite spot in all the world. Once the staff told me she had a wonderful day playing with three dachshunds. Another day, they say that she played very nicely with another Westie, one who had lost a leg to cancer. They always tell me they have loved having her there and that she's a wonderful dog. Proud parent that I am, I always believe them.

When I come for her in the evening, the staff has learned to allow me to settle the bill before bringing Ramona out. When the door opens and she catches sight of me, she is just as enthusiastic in greeting me as she was in coming to Miss Kitty's in the morning. She becomes a leaping, twirling, cavorting bundle of white fur until I put her in the car and we turn away from Miss Kitty's. Always an affectionate dog, her affection knows no bounds in these few brief moments of reunion.

Soon she settles down, and usually even before we reach the Franklin Pike, not more than a mile away, she is beginning to doze on the seat beside me. By the time we reach home, she is sleeping the sleep of the exhausted but perfectly contented dog. She may wake for a drink of water or for her milk bones at bedtime, but she sleeps often long into the next day, restoring her strength and dreaming dreams of the joys that have been hers at Miss Kitty's.

Ramona, The Wonder Puppy

Succeeding years with Ramona seem to fuel rather than slake the fires of my imagination. In my own fantasy life, I find that daydreams about Ramona and her accomplishments have now generally displaced those concerning my own life. I usually fancy her performing feats that might not be impossible for her, but ones that would be a stretch for any dog to perform, even one with her sterling qualities. These plays of imagination bring me much satisfaction.

For example, last year when our son and his fiancée

were planning their wedding, I began to imagine that Ramona might serve as ring bearer. I could envision her, snowy clean and newly groomed, with a collar of flowers, walking up the aisle behind two chimerical flower girls. The rings would be suspended from a gold chain hanging around her neck, and when the moment came for the giving of rings, she would stand up on her hind legs so that the minister could remove the gold chain and rings.

I began to imagine that Ramona might serve as ringbearer.

When I considered this in the cold light of day, I felt certain that Ramona could never be trained to fulfill such a role. She is very gregarious, so that, instead of walking sedately down the aisle, she would insist on greeting all the guests along the way. Furthermore, in her impatience to greet each one, she would rise up on her hind legs again and again before the appointed moment for the giving of rings. And, once the rings were lifted from her, she would most surely not stand quietly awaiting the recessional. Instead, she would likely run down from the altar, and leap up on the front pew to sit between Ann and me.

Our son dampened my enthusiasm for this scenario even more when he told me that he had actually attended a wedding in which a dog served as ring bearer. In that instance, the bride, a professional dog trainer, had schooled one of her dogs to fulfill this exact role, so that it went off smoothly. Harwell also observed, however, that the dog's performance had to some extent taken attention away from the bride and groom. All eyes had been glued to the dog.

I decided then to focus my imagination on more dog-like roles for Ramona. The next image comes to me in a movie theater, where the film showing is a Metro-Goldwyn-Mayer movie. As usual, just before the film begins, the M-G-M symbol appears on the screen, with the lion couchant yet roaring in the center. Now, I think, that is a role that Ramona could play. She might easily take the place of the lion in that symbol, with one paw draped casually over the ledge. The only problem that I can foresee would be persuading Ramona to bark on cue, or indeed, getting her to bark at all. She would be far more likely to yawn than to

I focused on more dog-like roles for Ramona.

bark, and I doubt M-G-M would want a yawning dog to introduce their pictures, even though this might be an accurate foretaste of the film.

I dream on. We are spending a weekend at our country place in Beersheba Springs. Further fancy leads me to a telephone call there on a Saturday afternoon, alerting us that two young children visiting at a neighboring cottage cannot be found. We are frightened because there is a precipitous drop from the ledge that borders the bluff side of all our houses, and if the children should have fallen from the bluff, they are, at the very least, certain to be seriously injured. I envisage that Ann and I join in the search, along with neighbors and the rescue squad. We scour every foot of the bluff for the children, to no avail. Dark approaches, demanding the day's end of the search through the dangerous terrain. As Ann and I sadly wend our way home, we despair of finding the children. Suddenly, as we arrive home, we discover that Ramona too is missing. Knowing that she will return, even from a distance, if we whistle, call her loudly, and promise a treat, we summon her home. There is no response. I set out to find her.

As I reach the road high up behind our property, I perceive, ever so faintly, the bark of a dog. Rushing back to the house to tell Ann, I alert her to bring a lantern and every flashlight. We renew our search. Up on the road again, we listen but hear no sound. In a moment it reappears, soft and steady now, a gentle bark. We cross the road, move through dense woods, cautious now. It's suddenly colder and darker. We can see nothing beyond the circle of lights we carry. Thick underbrush claws at us. We make slow progress. Even so, the barking grows louder. As we stumble over stones that appear to have once been the foundation of a house long gone, we can see a patch of white. It's Ramona, now barking loudly, coming through the darkness. Rejoicing in discovering her, we turn towards home. But she does not follow. She sits calmly, waiting. As we turn again to leave, she begins to bark, to run in circles, finally to stop at the edge of a deep hole. We hear another sound, the distinct

In a moment it reappears, soft and steady now, a gentle bark.

sound of crying. Casting our lights into the hole, we see two children, fallen apparently into an old cistern that must have served the abandoned house. The children are cold, frightened, and hungry, but they appear uninjured.

Hooray! The children have been rescued, and are unharmed. The Wells' dog found them. Ramona is a heroine! Everyone wants to cheer her, to pay her homage. To honor her, the town elders elect her Queen of the Fourth of July Parade, the first nonhuman to be given this honored position. In preparation for this important event, we buy for her a red, white, and blue collar, and we bathe her with special care on the evening before. On the morning of the Fourth, she is bedecked with a small crown of gold, securely fixed by an elastic band under her chin. She sits regally atop the bright red fire truck leading the parade. The citizenry of the town and the visitors who line State Route 56 all applaud Ramona.

Fancy takes me to another scene. We are in Washington, where Queen Elizabeth II is paying a state visit. I've brought Ramona so that she may have a glimpse of the Queen in the great parade along Pennsylvania Avenue, scheduled for tomorrow. Ramona has always shown a surprising interest in royalty, so I decided that we must take her along on this rare opportunity to view Queen Elizabeth. We rise at dawn, so as to find a choice place along the parade route. How fortunate we are to find a spot just behind the restraining ropes, with an unobstructed view. The wait is long, and Ramona begins to grow restive just as we hear the band strike up from the White House Lawn. As the music grows louder, and the Queen moves nearer, Ramona, in a flash, leaps from my arms to confront a disheveled man, furtively hiding a package, and standing close to us. Though she does not attack him, she barks furiously, running in quick circles around him, so as to hold him in one spot. I try to grab her, to no avail. The man who is the object of her barking at first appears embarrassed, then frightened, as he bolts away.

In a moment secret service men surround him.

In a moment secret service men surround and search him. They find not a gun, but a plastic container filled with emerald green paint. He had planned to sully the Queen's garments and disrupt the celebration with this ugly display of Irish color and solidarity.

The efficient secret service dispatches the culprit before the Queen and her entourage arrive at our place of waiting. We have a wonderfully close view as the open limousine passes by. I am excited. Ramona is ecstatic, dancing on her hind legs, front paws waving. Although it is uncharacteristic, I believe that the Queen actually winks at Ramona.

We are late getting back to our room. Since I had some difficulty securing accommodations for Ramona in Washington, we are staying at a small, nondescript motel in Rockville, Maryland. As no taxis could be found near the parade route, we have had several long bus rides and hikes before returning.

Having just settled into the room's only comfortable

chair, I hear the phone ringing. The caller announces that he is Equerry to the Queen, and that he is calling on her behalf. After her staff had informed her of Ramona's brave acts of confronting the culprit during the day's parade, the Queen wishes to meet Ramona and to present her with a medal. The President has kindly offered use of the White House Rose Garden for the ceremony, and a conveyance will call for us at nine-thirty the following morning, if that time is convenient with Ramona. I sleep little that night. After bathing and brushing Ramona, I think constantly of the events of the next day, my mind racing with anticipation.

The Queen wishes to meet Ramona.

When morning finally arrives, Ramona and I arise early and look our best when the British ambassador's large Daimler arrives precisely at nine-thirty to take us to the White House. Once past security, we are ushered to the Rose Garden, where two chairs have been set up near a small podium, and we are asked to sit for a few minutes to await the Queen's arrival. As I hold Ramona on my lap, I become aware that she and I are the only ones present, aside from a bank of television and news camerapersons and reporters.

Only a few moments later, the Queen arrives, accompanied by six attendants and by the President and First Lady. She graciously makes a few kind remarks expressing gratitude to Ramona for having saved her from "grave embarrassment" on the previous day. She then asks Ramona to come forward to receive her medal.

At this point I put Ramona down, whereupon she scampers towards the Queen and stands looking up to her. An equerry hands the medal suspended on a ribbon to the Queen, who bends to place the ribbon around Ramona's neck. At this point, Ramona suddenly lifts her head and begins to lick the Queen's fingers. At first the Queen is surprised, but then she begins to smile and to pat Ramona. The television cameras record it all, and in the evening every network shows that rare moment displaying the Queen's congeniality.

Every network shows that rare moment displaying the Queeen's congeniality.

The scene changes to a final one for me. The setting is

St. George's Episcopal Church, where my funeral has just been held. Ramona has sat patiently throughout the service on the row beside Ann and our children. Now the officiant has pronounced the benediction, and the attendants begin to move the coffin down the center aisle. Suddenly Ramona jumps down and follows, head bowed, eyes downcast. She walks alone, nearest my body, ahead of the other family members, isolated in her grief. Kings and heroes have riderless horses to follow them to their graves. I have Ramona. Who is the more fortunate?

MORE ABOUT RAMONA

If you would like to know more about Ramona,
please contact:

BACKBONE PRESS
Box 58153
Nashville, TN 37205-8153
email: backbone@backbonepress.com
http://www.backbonepress.com

A Note on the type

This book is set in Weiss Roman, a typeface designed in
1928 by Emil R. Weiss for the Bauer Type Foundry, and later
cut into type by the Monotype Corporation. It is based on
the work of sixteenth-century type designers and its strong
calligraphic strokes convert well to
the digital version used here.

Book design by Gary Gore